Princess Ariel loved nothing more than to dream about life in the human world. But her father, King Triton, ruler of all the merfolk who live deep down in the sea, had forbidden all his subjects to visit the surface. He thundered to his daughters, "Humans are barbarians. I don't want to see you wind up on one of their hooks!"

But Ariel secretly defied her father and often swam to the surface to bask in the warmth of the sun's rays. This one morning was no different.

1

Ariel had awakened early and slipped out of the coral palace. It was going to be a beautiful day and she didn't want to miss any of it. She swam up from the deep blue of the bottom, through the greenish middle sea, up to the surface where the water was usually a warm, bright blue. This morning, however, the sea raged icy green. Ariel burst through the surface and shivered as huge icebergs glittered nearby. It was wintertime.

"Scuttle! Oh, Scuttle...where are you?" Ariel looked for the zany seagull who was teaching her all about human things, but she didn't see him anywhere. Instead, a large white pelican swooped down and settled on a chunk of floating ice. She smiled at the mermaid. "You won't find your friend at sea on a day like this, my dear. He's gone to land. It's almost Christmas!"

"Christmas? What's Christmas?" But the pelican flew away.

Ariel swam back to the palace. She had to find out about Christmas and she knew just who to ask. Before becoming the Royal Court Composer, Sebastian had travelled all around the sea.

The tiny crab was in his music room, writing his latest sea symphony. "Ariel, what are you doing here? Your music lesson is tomorrow! You feelin' all right, child?"

"I'm fine, Sebastian. I was just wondering about...Christmas."

"Christmas! Oh, man, what a happy time, full of de carols and de Christmas trees and dey give de gifts and, most importantly, everybody got de good will toward each other. Why, back in Jamaica—" Then he eyed her suspiciously. "Ariel, Christmas, it's a <u>human</u> holiday. Why do you want to know?"

"Oh, I, uh, heard some of the tuna talking about it. You know what chatterboxes they are...I'd better go...practice—see you tomorrow! Thanks, Sebastian."

Ariel glided to a small hole in the sea rock, hidden by sea ferns that waved to and fro with the current. She parted the ferns and peeked inside. "Oh, Flounder—what a sleepyfish you are. Wake up! We've got to go to the grotto!"

"Aw, Ariel, it's so early!" But the little fish rubbed his eyes and swam loyally after his best friend.

Inside the secret grotto where Ariel kept her treasured collection of artifacts from the human world, Flounder watched curiously as the little mermaid searched through a sea chest. "It must be here ... somewhere ..." Triumphantly, Ariel held up a book. She pointed to the pictures. "This must be what Sebastian was talking about. Here's a tree, and presents, and people singing! Oh, Flounder, it looks like so much fun! Wouldn't it be wonderful if we could celebrate Christmas too?"

"Gee, Ariel, that sounds great! What do we do?" Flounder whirled excitedly. Then he stopped and fluttered his fins. "Uh, we won't have to go very far, will we?"

"We'll make everything right here! It'll be fantastic!" Ariel stretched out on the sand and studied the pictures. "Now think, Flounder. Where are we going to find a Christmas tree?"

Back in the palace gardens, Ariel and Flounder eyed the seatrees that surrounded King Triton's castle. "What about one of these, Ariel?"

"They're pretty . . . but they don't look like Christmas trees. And you know how Daddy feels about human things. He'd be furious so this has to be our secret. We need to find something we can take back to the grotto. Come on, Flounder, let's go!"

Their search took them far away from the palace to where the water grew dark and cold. "Uh, Ariel. I don't think we're going to find any Christmas trees around here. Maybe we ought to go home now."

"Just a little farther…" Ariel kept right on swimming until she rounded a bend in the sea rock. "Flounder, come here! Look what I found!"

Flounder dashed after her. "I'm coming, Ariel!"

There, growing in a patch of bright sunlight that filtered down from the surface high above, was a magnificent grove of coral trees. They were all sorts of fantastic shapes, but right in the middle was one that looked just like a Christmas tree! Ariel spun around happily. "It's just the right size." She tugged at the dead coral tree and pulled it free of the sandy ground. Together Ariel and Flounder carried it back to the secret grotto.

In the days that followed, the two friends searched the palace grounds for decorations to put on their Christmas tree. Ariel gathered tiny sea-plants from the gardens and nestled them among the coral branches. Flounder found some pretty colored sea-vines to drape over the tree, but it still didn't look like the Christmas tree in the picture.

Ariel shook her head. "Something's not right. Maybe we need more shiny things!"

So they gathered sea crystals and seashells, and even oyster
shells that had been left behind when the oysters moved away.
Ariel cracked open the empty shells, admiring the beautiful colors
inside. "Oh, these'll be perfect."

"Look, Ariel! I found another one. But this one's stuck…tight…
ouch!" A mussel shell slammed shut on Flounder's fin! He tugged
and tugged until he finally pulled free. "I guess somebody's still
living there."

13

At last Ariel's satchel was full. Surely now they had enough pretty ornaments for the tree and they hurried back to the grotto. They were just about to tug on the rock that hid the secret entrance when suddenly Sebastian popped up from behind a reef. "Where are you goin' with dat stuff?"

"Oh, Sebastian! Um…we were just…uh—"

"It's my stuff, Sebastian. And, um, Ariel's helping me carry it to my, uh, rock. Yeah, that's it. It's my treasure." The little fish grinned at Ariel.

Sebastian's eyes narrowed, but he shook his head as he scuttled off. "I know you two. You're up to somet'ing. An' one of dese days, I'm gonna find out what!"

All afternoon Ariel and Flounder decorated the coral Christmas tree. The branches sparkled and glittered with the gleaming shells and—just as if they knew this was something special—the sea-flowers put forth their brightest blossoms.

As Ariel hung up a wreath she'd fashioned from seaweeds and pearls, Flounder gazed at it with admiration. "It looks just like Christmas, Ariel!"

Ariel looked at the tree. "I don't know, Flounder. It's not as much fun as I expected. Something is still wrong."

"I don't think so, Ariel. I bet if you ask anyone, they'll say it's a perfect Christmas tree!"

"That's it, Flounder! There's more to Christmas than just a tree! Sebastian said Christmas was all about good will toward others. That means our Christmas should be shared with everyone!"

Ariel clapped her hands in glee. "Let's make some presents and surprise everyone!"

Ariel decided to give her prettiest hair-comb to Aquata, her favorite shell-mirror to Andrina, a bouquet of sea-flowers to Arista, and a pearl to Adela. "I'll make an oyster-shell purse for Attina and read Alana bedtime stories every night for a week!"

It was easy finding the right present for Flounder. She picked out his favorite human object — a tiny telescope he liked to look through — and wrapped it up. She also wrote out a promise to Sebastian not to miss any of her music lessons for a month. Then she thought about her father. "Oh dear. He doesn't like anything human. He probably isn't going to like Christmas at all." But Ariel was determined to share her undersea Christmas with everybody. Finally, she selected a beautiful conch shell for King Triton.

Late that night, after everyone in the palace had gone to sleep, Ariel and Flounder sneaked into the great hall with the coral Christmas tree. "Ssh, we can't make any noise."

"I know that—Ariel, I'm not a guppy anymore!"

All night long they decorated the great hall, working by the soft green light of phosphor lamps just bright enough to see by but not bright enough to wake anyone.

Along the amber windowsills Ariel hung stockings made from fishnets and filled them with tiny trinkets and pretty shells. Once again, the little mermaid and Flounder decorated the coral Christmas tree. The flowering plants waved softly in the current, sending up tiny bubbles that nestled in the coral, sparkling like diamonds in the night.

Just before dawn, Ariel crowned the coral tree with a five-pointed sea-star and Flounder placed their presents underneath.

As morning's first light filtered down into the palace, Sebastian clattered into the great hall! "Jumping jellyfish! It's Christmas!" Ariel beamed as her sisters swam in. "Surprise!"

Sebastian laughed. "Man, I didn't expect to see another Christmas ever again! Just like in Jamaica! Merry Christmas, everybody. Merry Christmas!"

Suddenly, King Triton swept into the hall. "What's the meaning of this?! Ariel! What have you done?!"

"It's Christmas, Daddy. I know it's human, but it's about making people feel good. And it makes me feel so good to share it with all of you. I tried to keep it a secret but I just couldn't! There's so much I want to give!"

"She's got de spirit of Christmas all right!" Sebastian sidled over to the king. "Your majesty, dis is a time of good will toward everyone!"

King Triton glared at the little crab. "You, too, Sebastian?"

Ariel handed King Triton the beribboned conch shell. "This is for
you, Daddy. So you can hear the sounds of your whole kingdom."
The king held the conch shell to his ear. He could hear the sea, full
of the joyful sounds of his happy subjects. Triton looked at Ariel,
her face shining with love and hope. He smiled. "So be it.
Christmas is a time of good will toward all!"

Sebastian grinned. "And a time for de Christmas carols! Listen,
everybody! We got some songs to sing!"